Making a Difference

Teaching Children Kindness, Character, and Purpose

CHERI J. MEINERS, M.ED.

Illustrated by: Pascale Lafond

Mango Publishing Group
2850 Douglas Road, 3rd Floor
Coral Gables, FL 33134 USA
info@mango.bz

For special orders, quantity sales, course adoptions and corporate sales, please email the publisher at sales@mango.bz. For trade and wholesale sales, please contact Ingram Publisher Services at customer.service@ingramcontent.com or +1.800.509.4887.

Making a Difference: Teaching Children Kindness, Character, and Purpose

Library of Congress Cataloging
ISBN: (print) 978-1-63353-598-5, (ebook) 978-1-63353-597-8
Library of Congress Control Number: 2017949541
BISAC category code : JNF053200 JUVENILE NONFICTION / Social Topics / Values & Virtues

Printed in the United States of America

"This invaluable resource...empowers children to be their best selves and challenges them to make a real world difference every day."

— Mary Jane Weiss, Ph.D., Director, Douglass Developmental Disabilities Center, Rutgers University and co-author of *Reaching Out, Joining In*

I want to do things that matter!

I look for ways that I can make a difference.

When I make a good choice,
it's not an accident.

I do it 'on purpose'.

8

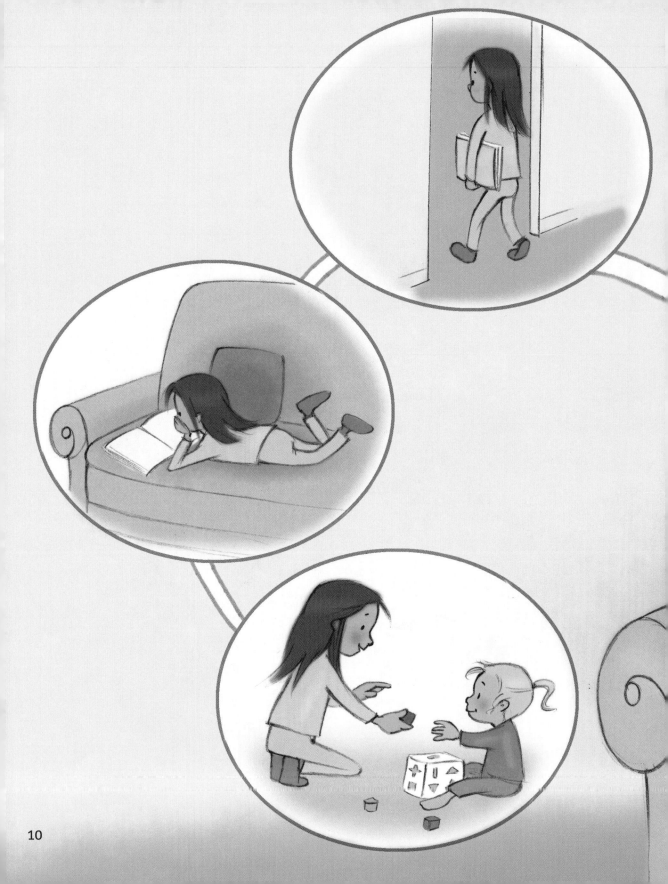

I imagine lots of choices.

Then, I decide what seems best.

When I do good, and I'm kind,
it feels right.

I can do hard things.

**I feel good about myself
when I do things that make a difference.**

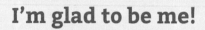

I'm glad to be me!

And I enjoy the people and
things around me.

18

Even little things have a purpose.

I look for what's good and beautiful.
And I usually find it!

I like to do my best.

I put my heart into things
that are important to me.

When I do something well,

I feel that what I do matters.

Especially when I share it!

We all have a story and a purpose.

I want to listen, and show respect.

I'll keep trying to do good,

and to be kind.

And I'll be positive, and find good in things.

I'm living with purpose.

I can think about what someone wants,
and how I can help.

When I care about people,
my world gets bigger.

I can do things that make a difference.

In my own way,
I'm making the world a little better.

Activity ideas for
MAKING A DIFFERENCE

It is rewarding and fulfilling to children when they know that what they do matters and makes a difference to someone. A sense of purpose can guard against feelings of helplessness and depression. It can also lead to improved sleep and physical health, and predicts long-term good health. A clear sense of purpose often sparks a desire to help others and to make a difference by being involved in causes greater than oneself.

Read this book often with your child or group of children. Once children are familiar with the book, refer to it as a tool to teach and reinforce these three common themes that can build a sense of purpose.

1. **Be positive**—develop attitudes such as courage, hope and resilience
2. **Be kind**—build relationships and care about others
3. **Do good**— learn, achieve and share

'Making a Difference' Bulletin Board

Materials: poster paper; drawing paper; crayons and markers

Directions: With a marker, write the formula below on poster paper. Discuss the concepts together. Talk about how doing good, being kind and being positive can bring purpose to one's life, and make a difference for others. Then ask children to draw a picture of an important relationship, something they have accomplished, or a time they have been positive. Display pictures under your sign.

Be Positive + Be Kind + Do Good = Making a Difference

1. **Be Positive**—*attitude.* As children are positive and develop attitudes of courage and hope in facing difficulties, they will feel a greater a sense of purpose. Their strength of character can make a difference for others, as well.

2. **Be Kind**—*relationships.* As children show kindness to others, their circle of influence increases, as does their ability to make a difference for someone else.

3. **Do Good**—*achievement.* As children learn, achieve new things and develop interests and talents, their gifts can lift themselves and others.

As you read each spread, you might ask children:

What is happening in this picture?
What is the main idea?
How do you think this person feels?
How would you feel if you were this person?

Here are additional questions you might discuss as you read:

- What does it mean to do something 'on purpose'? Can a person do something nice 'on purpose'? Why or why not?

- What is something that's important to you? Why?

- What is a good choice you have made?

- What is something hard you have done? What do you like to work hard at?

- What do you think it means to 'put your heart into' something? When have you done that?

- What is something you enjoy doing?

- What is something that you do well? How do you feel when you do it?

- What is something you can share with someone else? How does that make you feel?

- What is something that you like about yourself? What do you like about your life?

- What is something you are grateful for?

- Think of a person in your family, or one of your friends. What is a way that you can encourage or respect that person?

- What do you like to help people with?

- What is something you have done to help someone else? How did it feel?

- What is a way that you can make the world a little better?

Digging Deep to Find Purpose

Materials: A large plastic container with a lid; clean dry rice or birdseed, enough to fill several inches of the container; several small household items such as those listed below; a large spoon or scoop.

Preparation: Put the small items in the container, and cover them with a few inches of rice or seed.

Directions: Let a child dig until an item is uncovered.

Level 1: As a child holds up the item, ask the children, "What is the purpose of this item?" (For example, if the item is a book, the purpose is "to be read".)

Level 2: After children can respond to the Level 1 questions, play again and ask these questions: "How can this make a difference for you?" or "How could you make a difference for someone else by using this?" You may need to prompt them at first. (For example, "I learn new things when I read books.")

Three types of purpose (or ways to make a difference) are:

    a) Be Positive. I can have a good attitude about it.
    b) Be Kind. I can help someone with it.
    c) Do Good. I can do something useful with it.

Here are some examples of items and responses for Level 1 and Level 2 question.

	Level 1	Level 2
book	to be read	I can learn new things.
fork	to eat	I can eat dinner with my family, and talk around the table.
comb	to comb hair	I can take care of myself when I comb my own hair.
card	to send to someone	I can write and send it to cheer someone who is sick.
ball	to play with	I can play a game with a friend.
crayon	to color	I can explain how I feel when I draw a picture.
a quarter	to buy something	I can save my allowance for something I want to buy.
scissors	to cut	I can cut paper and ribbon to wrap a present.

Making a Difference (through attitude, caring, and achievement).

The following activities can help children find ways to make a difference for themselves and others. Take time to incorporate some of these ideas into your child's schedule. You may wish to post and discuss the following sentences. Have children repeat the phrases and focus on them in the settings below.

Be Positive. I can have a good attitude.
Be Kind. I can help someone.
Do Good. I can do something useful.

Ponder: Slowing down and taking time to be thoughtful, to ponder and contemplate are useful tools for children to process thoughts and feelings. They can take time to remember what they feel grateful for; plan upcoming activities; or evaluate how they might act in a relationship. Children can ponder ways that they can make a difference as they take time to think about the things that have meaning and give a sense of purpose to their lives.

Journal: Keeping a journal can help children evaluate the activities of the day as they are recorded. They can focus on the things accomplished, the relationships enjoyed, or how to courageously face struggles. You may let children dictate their thoughts for you to write, or you might help them write by putting difficult words in a personal dictionary for those who can write. They may wish to add their own illustration.

Nature: When possible, take nature walks in a park or grow a potted plant in a window. Being in nature can relax the mind, promote awareness of one's surroundings, and can be healing and helpful in sensing one's importance and place in the world.

Play: Unstructured play is essential for children's physical, mental, social and emotional health. A balance of undirected play is beneficial to offset the serious nature of school, homework, chores and other meaningful adult-directed activities the child may be involved in. Through play children also have the opportunity to explore the world and its challenges in a nonthreatening way. This, in itself, is a purposeful activity. Natural interaction with others gives opportunities to practice doing good, being kind, and being positive.

You can find more Making A Difference activity ideas by visiting: cherijmeiners.net

Author Bio

Cheri J. Meiners, M.Ed., is the author of the award-winning *Learning to Get Along* series and the *Being the Best Me* series for young children. Cheri has her master's degree in elementary education and gifted education and is a former first-grade teacher. She also taught education classes at Utah State University and has supervised student teachers. Cheri and her husband, David, have six children and eight grandchildren. They live in Laurel, Maryland.